Waldo, Tell Me About God

WALDO, TELL ME ABOUT GOD

First published in the USA by C. Gibson Company, Norwalk, CT06856.

Commonwealth addition by Word (UK) Ltd. 1990.

Printed and bound in Singapore by Times Offset Pte Ltd

ISBN 0-85009-278-7

WORD PUBLISHING

WORD (UK) Ltd
Milton Keynes, England

WORD AUSTRALIA
Kilsyth, Victoria, Australia
STRUIK CHRISTIAN BOOKS (PTY) LTD
Maitland, South Africa
ALBY COMMERCIAL ENTERPRISES PTE LTD
Balmoral Road, Singapore
CHRISTIAN MARKETING NEW ZEALAND LTD
Havelock North, New Zealand
JENSCO LTD
Hong Kong
SALVATION BOOK CENTRE
Malaysia

Waldo, Tell Me About God

by Hans Wilhelm

Word Publishing
Milton Keynes
England

One sunny afternoon Michael and
his best friend, Waldo, were taking a
walk.

"It's a beautiful world that God
gave us, isn't it?" asked Waldo.

"Who is God?" asked Michael.

"Well," said Waldo, "God is Father to us all. God made everything— you and me, the plants, the animals, the rocks…."

"Did God make the sun?" asked Michael as he looked up at the sky. "And the clouds?"

"Yes, He did. And He made the moon and all the stars, too."

"Why did He make all this for us?" asked Michael.

Waldo put his arm around his friend and answered. "God gave us all these gifts because He loves us. He wants you to enjoy them with Him and share them with others."

"But what if I don't want to share? What if I do naughty things? Will God stop loving me?" asked Michael.

"No!" laughed Waldo. "God loves you even if you do naughty things. Love can never hurt you. Only by our own actions do we punish ourselves."

Michael was puzzled. "What do you mean?" he asked.

"Watch," said Waldo as he picked up Michael's toy boomerang which was lying in the grass. "What happens when I throw it?"

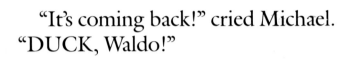

"It's coming back!" cried Michael.
"DUCK, Waldo!"

The two friends ran as fast as they could.

"Wow, that was close," said Michael as the boomerang whizzed by.

"See what I mean, Michael? Our actions can be just like a boomerang. So can our thoughts and words. The hurt and pain that we give to others come back to us sooner or later."

"But if I've made a mistake, isn't there anything I can do about it?"

"God will help you," replied Waldo. "You can turn to Him for help."

"How?" asked Michael.

"When you are truly sorry for what you did wrong you must ask for forgiveness and try very hard not to do it again. Then God may take your pain away and fill you with His love."

Michael and Waldo stopped to sit on a grassy spot at the top of the hill. They could see the beautiful valley all around them.

"God's love is in me?" Michael asked.

"God sends His love to make you strong and to help you. It is His love that keeps everything and everyone alive. Nothing can exist without God's love."

"And through His love, God is always with us wherever we are!" said Waldo as he flung out his arms. "He's in everything we see: the flowers, the stars, the sky. God is even in you and me!"

"Listen!" whispered Waldo.
"Can you *hear* God's love in the bird's song?"

Michael was very, very quiet. He wasn't sure....

"Look at these flowers, Michael.
Can you *smell* God's love?"
   Michael sniffed deeply. But he still
wasn't sure....
   While Waldo and Michael were
smelling the flowers, a family of
rabbits hopped over to join them.

Waldo picked up a little rabbit.
"Can't you *feel* God's love, Michael?"
Michael stroked the rabbit's
soft pink ear. He was beginning
to understand.

Michael and Waldo stopped to rest under a tree laden with fat red cherries. They helped themselves.

"Even the food we eat is a gift from God," said Waldo. "God's love nourishes you like good food does."

Michael was thoughtful for a moment. "I can see and feel and smell and hear God's love. He is all around me. He must love me very much."

"He does," said Waldo. "And until now, you've seen only a tiny part of His power and love. But He wants you to know Him even better."

"How?" asked Michael.

"By loving Him more than anything or anyone else."

"You mean even more than I love you?"

"Oh, yes! Much, much more," said Waldo with a smile, as he lifted Michael onto his shoulders.

"That will be hard to do!" cried Michael.

"No it won't," replied Waldo. "Through His love, God also lives in you and me. He's in everything. So when you love Him in a flower, in an animal, in a rock, in a friend and even in a beautiful sunset—then it becomes so easy!"

Michael was very quiet on the walk home. He had a lot to think about.

That evening, as Waldo helped Michael get ready for bed, the two friends talked some more.

"Do you know what God's best gift is?" asked Michael as Waldo tucked the blanket under his chin.

"What?"

"You," said Michael sleepily. "My friend."

"When we love each other, we are very close to God, aren't we Michael?"